W9-BDO-297

SAVING

Sweetness

DIANE STANLEY

ILLUSTRATED BY
G. BRIAN KARAS

PUFFIN BOOKS

PUFFIN BOOKS
Published by the Penguin Group
Penguin Putnam Books for Young Readers, 345 Hudson Street, New York, New York 10014, U.S.A.
Penguin Books Ltd, 27 Wrights Lane, London W8 5TZ, England
Penguin Books Australia Ltd, Ringwood, Victoria, Australia
Penguin Books Canada Ltd, 10 Alcorn Avenue, Toronto, Ontario, Canada M4V 3B2
Penguin Books (N.Z.) Ltd, 182-190 Wairau Road, Auckland 10, New Zealand

Penguin Books Ltd, Registered Offices: Harmondsworth, Middlesex, England

First published in the United States of America by G. P. Putnam's Sons,
a division of Penguin Putnam Books for Young Readers, 1996
Published by Puffin Books, a division of Penguin Putnam Books for Young Readers, 2001

9 10 8

Text copyright © Diane Stanley, 1996
Illustrations copyright © G. Brian Karas, 1996
All rights reserved

THE LIBRARY OF CONGRESS HAS CATALOGED THE G. P. PUTNAM'S SONS EDITION AS FOLLOWS:
Stanley, Diane. Saving Sweetness / by Diane Stanley; illustrated by G. Brian Karas.   p.   cm.
Summary: The sheriff of a dusty western town rescues Sweetness, an unusually
resourceful orphan, from nasty old Mrs. Sump and her terrible orphanage.
[1. Orphans—Fiction. 2. West (U.S.)—Fiction. 3. Humorous stories.] I. Karas, G. Brian, ill. II. Title.
PZ7.S7869SAV 1996 [E]—dc20 95-10621 CIP AC
ISBN 0-399-23645-1

Puffin Books ISBN 978-0-698-11767-9

Printed in the United States of America

For Dad and Claire, a warm Texas howdy–D.S.

For JJ and David, Scott and Ava–G.B.K.

Out in the hottest, dustiest part of town is an orphanage run by a female person nasty enough to scare night into day. She goes by the name of Mrs. Sump, though I doubt there ever was a Mr. Sump on accounta she looks like somethin' the cat drug in and the dog wouldn't eat. I heard that Mrs. Sump doesn't much like seein' the orphans restin' or havin' any fun, so she puts 'em to scrubbin' the floor with toothbrushes. Even the ittiest, bittiest orphan, little Sweetness. So one day, Sweetness hit the road.

I found out right away because Mrs. Sump came bustin'
into Loopy Lil's Saloon, hollerin' like a banshee.

"Sheriff!" she yelled (that's me). "That provokin' little
twerp—I mean that dear child, Sweetness, done escaped—
I mean, disappeared! And I'm fit to be tied, worryin' about
that pore thang all pink and helpless, wanderin' lost on the
plains and steppin' on scorpions and fallin' into holes and
such. You gotta bring her back alive—er, I mean, *safe*—before
she runs into *Coyote Pete!*"

That did it. Scorpions were one thing. But Coyote Pete is
as mean as an acre of rattlesnakes, and the toughest, ugliest
desperado in the West.

So I got my star and I buckled on my gun belt and headed west. It was hot as blazes. Seemed like the wind was too tired to blow. Then it got hotter. Hours passed, and what with the sun beatin' down on me, I commenced to feel thirsty. That was when I realized that it woulda been prudent to bring along some water. After some more hours, I begun to stagger with the thirst, and the next thing I knowed, I was plopped down in the dirt. Fortunately, I was in the shade of a big cactus, so I decided to stay there for a spell to catch my breath.

Next thing I knew, I felt this cool, delicious water tricklin'
over my tongue. I popped open my eyes, and there, just a shadow
against the sun, was little Sweetness and her big canteen!

As soon as I was watered up enough to make words come out of my mouth, I said, "Why, Sweetness, thank heaven I've saved you!" And she said, "Yes, sir. Thank you."

That little orphan is just as cute as a speckled pup under a wagon!

"Now I've come to take you home," says I.

"I don't want to go home," says she. "I'm tired of scrubbin' floors with a toothbrush."

"What can't be cured must be endured," I told her. Now, I thought this was very wise advice, but the orphan didn't seem to think so, 'cause she lit off like she was tryin' to catch yesterday.

This day was goin' from bad to worse. Now I was goin' to have to save that orphan again! Also, if you know anythin' about the desert, you know that when the sun goes down in all its glory, it starts to cool off, and then it gets right cold. Also, the snakes come out. So I headed off after Sweetness, all shiverin' and wishin' I'd brought a blanket.

I got to feelin' a trifle hungry, too. Seems like I was
wanderin' around among the snakes and the rocks for a
coon's age, till I was so tuckered out I just curled up against
a bush and went to sleep. Pretty soon I commenced to
dream that I was home with my own dear mama, sittin'
'round the fire all toasty warm and she was cookin' somethin'
nice. Then I woke up and there was the orphan and a camp-
fire, and that little tyke was a-toastin' marshmallows.

"Want one?" says she. Well, doesn't that just beat all?

"Now looky here, Sweetness," I says to her while I was gobblin' down them marshmallows, "this is the second time I done saved you, and I'd very much appreciate it if you'd *stay* saved. So we're gonna mosey on back to that there orphanage right now."

Well, I'll be darned if she didn't start to cry!

"Don't you like me?" she asked.

"Why, sure I do, honey! Ain't I saved you twice? There's nothin' to cry about."

But she went right on bawlin'. "I ain't got no ma," says she. "I ain't got no pa. All I got is Mrs. Sump and a toothbrush."

"Well, ain't no way to fix that lessen you gits adopted," I explained.

Then she smiled up in my face like she was expectin' me to say somethin' particular. It was too deep fer me.

"It sure is a dilemma," was all I could come up with to say. At which she threw up her little hands in the air and stomps off into the night.

"Dang!" says I. "Now you quit that! You really fry my patience." But I was gonna bring that orphan back if it harelipped the governor!

So there was the sun rising over
the plains, and there I was, feelin' like
somethin' that was chewed up and spit
out, tryin' to find one little orphan out
in the big, wild West.

Now here comes the excitin' part. I had gone fur enough to work up a good sweat, so I ambled over to a big rock so's I could stand in the shade. That's when I heard the sound. Just a little click, like a gun bein' cocked. I turned around and what'd I see but Coyote Pete, loaded for bear and givin' me a look that would freeze a cat. I had ta think fast.

"Coyote Pete," I told him, "you can see by the star on my chest that I is here to uphold the law. Now you can't go around shootin' folks and scarin' orphans, and I's here to arrest you."

Now it don't seem like he heard what I said, 'cause just as cool as you please he aimed his six-shooter right at my big silver star.

"Listen here, hamster brain," I says, "you're ridin' for a fall. You put down that there gun or I'm gonna knock you into the middle of next week. I'm gonna snatch you bald-headed. I'm gonna lock you up and throw away the key!"

And you know what he done? He made a sound like "thunk" and fell over backwards, laid out cold like a sacka feed. I scared him that bad! And who should show up just then but Sweetness. She took off her hair ribbons and we tied that varmint up bulletproof and pig tight.

"Now Sweetness," I told her, "I
ain't havin' no more of this runnin'
away. You can't go roamin' around
this here prairie with outlaws all over
the place. It's too dangerous. How
many times has I gotta save you?"

"If you was as smart as you is brave, you could figure out how to save me fer good," she said, lookin' me right in the eye. There we stood, havin' a kinda starin' contest.

"What you leadin' up to?" says I.

"Think," says she.

So I chewed on it awhile longer. "Do it have somethin' to do with adoptin'?"

"You're gettin' it," she says.

I was startin' to get a kinda pretty picture up in my head regardin' me and little Sweetness and a couple a rockin' chairs by the fire.

"Well, sweet child," I says to her, "I knows I's a rough character, but if you was to agree to it, *I* could adopt you."

"Pa!" says she, and she fell on me like Grandma on a chicken snake.

Then me and Sweetness rolled that
varmint all the way back to town.

Now here come the endin'. That very day I done signed them adoption papers.

Then that precious child told me about the seven other orphans and how their toothbrushes was worn down to little nubs with all that scrubbin'. So I adopted them, too.

As for Coyote Pete, we put him in jail and I got a big reward fer bringin' that varmint to justice. After a few years they let him out and put him in the custody of a parole officer. This was none other than Mrs. Sump, who, as you can see, was out of the orphan business. And I don't know how she done it, but she got that desperado to marry her, and now all he does is scrub that floor. And I can tell you, he jumps when she hollers frog.

And that's the truth.